The Legend of D'Woof-ta, The Little White Wolf

How the First Snow Came

By
Clifton E. Stine

Illustrations by
Dwight Nacaytuna

Dedicated to

Rayne and Conner

To order additional copies of this book, contact:
Xlibris
1-888-795-4274
www.Xlibris.com
Orders@Xlibris.com

In ages past when the two-legged beast had not yet learned to tame the free peoples of the forest, the hills, and the plains, there was only one unchanging season that embraced the lands. In that time the great sun rose every morning to warm the ground and bring light to the new earth and all its clans. One day was like the next. Except for the gentle rain showers that would occasionally wander in from the blue sea, the days never changed, and the nights were always cool and calm.

2

Mother Nature was the more compassionate of the First Parents. She brought forth all the clans of the free peoples and set them on the lands each in their own place. Father Time had molded the earth and sky, the forests and plains, and all the seas as dwellings for their children. In the early times Mother Nature loved the animals first while Father Nature loved his earth. In time both grew to cherish each other's work equally.

In those times all the animals roamed freely over the lands, but soon the plains and forests became filled and over crowded. The sick and weak as well as the old and feeble fed on the young grasses and drank the clear water. Father Time who was the wiser of the first parents saw that the free peoples needed another clan to keep their kinds strong and healthy. He knew that there was not enough for all. Something would have to be done so that only the strongest and fittest of the free people would share the gifts of the young world.

One bright star lit night Father Time walked out onto the grassy plain near the first of the bubbling springs. This fountain sprang from a crop of stones where the forest met the plains. The new born waters pooled in a shallow pond and then danced down the hill to a distant lake. Along the way fireflies drifted on the gentle wind flickering on and off as they chased the stream across the rolling plain. Father Time looked over the hills and streams and smiled. "This is a good place to bring forth the last clan," he said. So there between the forests and the plains where the water flowed into a sparkling pool Father Time brought forth the Mother Wolf.

Sitting by these clear waters, Father Time waited patiently for the rising moon and grasped its first rays of light in one hand. From the beams he wove a soft coat of fur. He in his other hand he took the strongest oak from the forest and molded a lean swift body with four strong legs. He found velvety moss from the shore of the flowing stream and gave it feet as quiet and soft as a morning breeze. He finally filled his hands with water from the spring just as it burst from the earth and stirred it with the first evening breeze. Father Time then commanded his form to drink, and the first of the new clan drank the life of the earth. So was the Great Mother Wolf born into the lands and forests of the young world.

On that first day Father Time spoke to the wolf and told her to only take the sick, the weak and the old so that the rich fields, forests, and streams would be used for the most good by the other free peoples. He told the mother wolf not to tell the free people of his charge so that all would be equally tested. One day the great wolf looked up at the sun and felt the warmth and light of its rays. She saw the other free peoples of the earth. The deer, the rabbits, the fish in the streams and the birds of the sky all had young of their own kind to help them in their work. But the great mother wolf had been alone from the beginning of her time. No one was there to help her. She was the only one of her clan. Her coat was the finest of fur that was given to change to the colors of the trees or grasses. This great gift was also the most feared by the other animals. They did not understand the wisdom of Father Time, and their fear of the great wolf grew daily. She was invisible to them in the forest and she was invisible to them on the plains. There was no place that the animals could feel safe. Father Time had not told the free animals that the Great Mother Wolf was forbidden from taking the healthy and strong members of the clan. So all the animals ran from the mother wolf, and all the animals were tested to find the fittest and most worthy to roam the fruitful valleys and hills of the new world.

The great wolf went then to Father Time and pointed to the forest, hills and plains that were given to her to roam. "I am only one, but you have given all the other free people helpers to aid them. Why must I be the only wolf, with no help? I travel the forest, the hills and the plains from dawn to dusk, without rest to do your bidding. And everyday the free peoples numbers increase while I am still only one. Will you give to me, Father Time, only what you have given to all the free people?" she begged.

Father Time looked on the Mother Wolf and knew that her task was great. She needed help to do what he had asked of her. "Go to your den," he said, "and when morning's first rays strike your face, you will have your helpers." The Great Wolf went to her den as she was told, and when the moon raised its silver halo above the far hills she fell into a deep sleep. That evening one wolf went into the den but instead of only one wolf rising to see the morning sun, five wolves awoke to new day. The Mother Wolf and her four new children. All the new wolves looked just like their mother except a little smaller. Only the youngest cub was different because he was also the smallest and the least noticed among his brother and sisters. His mother called him D'Woof-ta.

Now the Mother Wolf had lived along time and in her years she had taken on the colors of the earth. Her invisibility as she roamed through the lands made her task easier. Only in her den at dawn and dusk as day's light faded into dark could one see her true coat. It was a beautiful mixture of tans and grays with a sprinkling of black and white. She was a most magnificent animal. Her children were all the color of their mother. You could not tell them apart. But the other animals of the forest and plain saw that instead of one wolf, now there were five wolves to hunt them. So the animals of the forest and plains went to Mother Nature who they knew was gentler and kinder than Father Time and begged her take the Great Wolf's children away. Mother Nature could not undo what Father Time had willed, but because all the animals were grumbling so much, she had to do something.

After much thought she decided that the gift of invisibility that Father Time had given to the mother wolf was too great for her children. So Mother Nature decided to paint the new wolves different colors but not all the colors of the mother wolf so that the other animals of the clans could see them and run to safety. One night when all the wolf family was asleep Mother Nature sent her painted butterflies to their den to brush their colored wings against the young wolves and forever change their coats. The butterflies worked all night painting the young wolves, all but one. The smallest wolf lay in the corner of the den with a blanket of leaves covering him. At last, when the three cubs were painted and the butterfly princesses began to leave, their queen noticed a rustling of leaves in the corner and saw the last wolf. "What shall we do?" she cried. "We have used all our colors on the three cubs and have no more. Mother Nature will be very disappointed if all the cubs are not colored.

The young butterfly princesses looked at the littlest wolf, and after very much thought The queen said, "If we have no color, we'll just have to paint the last cub, no color." And so they did. In the morning when they rose again the mother wolf looked at her children and cried, "What has happened! You have all changed color, and your colors are so different from my colors that you'll never be able to hunt and eat. In the excitement all the wolves ran out into the sun to see what had happened to their brothers and sisters. The first-born sister has the colors of new sprouted grasses and tree bark just as the blossoms begin to bud before the leaves begin to grow. The second born brother has the colors of the full-grown forest with deep greens and grays. The third born sister has the colors of a golden tan harvest with a sprinkling of reds and oranges and the last-born brother was all white.

Now the animals complained that Mother Nature had tricked them and painted only some of the young wolves colors they could easily see. The clans that lived on plains complained about the harvest and tan colored wolf, and the clans that lived in the forest and hills complained about the deep green and tree bark colored wolf and those that lived in the meadows complained about the sprouting grass and blossoms colored wolf, but no one complained about the white wolf. D'Woof-ta was the last and smallest and now the most conspicuous member of his family.

The Mother Wolf now had help, but the help was only good for specific places. D'Woof-ta had no place! Try as hard as he could, on the plains he could not even catch a rabbit, and in the forest a mouse would see his white coat long before he could get near. The meadows were even worse. Birds and ground squirrels would squawk loudly when he came near. The little white wolf was getting very, very hungry.

In desperation D'Woof-ta went to see Father Time and showed him what Mother Nature had done. "Your help mate has painted all my brothers and sisters. They each are the color of a part of the lands and have home's to roam in while I have nowhere to live. Can you change my color so that I may have a chance to live as my brothers and sisters do?" he cried.

Father Time looked at the young wolf and sadly said that he cannot undo what Mother Nature has done, but he will try to make all things equal. So Father Time sat down by the stream that flowed between the plains and the forest and thought. The little white wolf laid down in front of him and watched intensely wondering what Father Time would do to make all things equal. Father Time thought all the rest of that day and all through the night and almost to high noon the next day. Then he got up and looked at D'Woof-ta and said, "I have an answer for you and all your clan." The little white wolf eagerly looked up at Father Time to see the wise old man gazing deep into his bright eyes.

Father Time then stood up by the first spring where the Great Mother Wolf was born. He reached down with his right hand and scooped up the bubbling water in his palm. With his left hand he raised his staff and pointed toward the blue sky. The air began to turn cold. He then tossed the magical waters into the air as high as he could. In that moment white flakes of lacy white frozen mist began to float down from the sky. The first snow had begun. Then Father Time said to the young wolf, "As my wife has colored you and all your brother and sisters, so I will give each of you your own time to rule the lands. To your first sister I give the spring, to your second brother I give the summer, to your second sister I give the fall and to you little D'Woof-ta I give the winter. And so it shall be from now until the end of time.

Printed in the United States
By Bookmasters